# Magic Pony

### Night-Time Adventure

Showjumping by moonlight! What could be more thrilling?

"Penelope Potter'd be furious if she found out I'd used her jumps without asking," whispered Natty, as with shining eyes she took hold of the reins and sprang on to Ned's back. Wellingtons and pyjamas disappeared and she was transformed into a rider with velvet hard hat, hacking jacket, jodhpurs and jodhpur boots.

Follow all of Natty and Ned's adventures!
Collect all the fantastic books in the
Magic Pony series:

# Magic Pony

## Night-Time Adventure

### ELIZABETH LINDSAY

*Illustrated by John Eastwood*

SCHOLASTIC

*For my uncle, R.W.H., with love.*

Scholastic Children's Books,
Commonwealth House, 1–19 New Oxford Street,
London WC1A 1NU, UK
a division of Scholastic Ltd
London ~ New York ~ Toronto ~ Sydney ~ Auckland

First published in the UK by Scholastic Ltd, 1997
This edition published in the UK by Scholastic Ltd, 2005

Text copyright © Elizabeth Lindsay, 1997
Illustrations copyright © John Eastwood, 1997

ISBN 0 439 95963 2

Printed and bound by Nørhaven Paperback A/S, Denmark

2 4 6 8 10 9 7 5 3

# Contents

# Chapter 1

## A Night-Time Surprise

Natty woke up suddenly and unexpectedly in the dark with something tickling her ear. It felt like the hairy feet of a spider and she quickly brushed it away. The tickling started again on her chin and warm air blew on her cheek. Pressing herself against the wall, she

reached the light switch at last. She
laughed when the light came on. It
wasn't a spider at all. Nothing like.

It was the tickling of pony whiskers and the blowing of warm pony breath. Ned had woken her, the beautiful chestnut pony who lived in the poster pinned to her bedroom wall. His gentle lips wobbled affectionately against her cheek. How lucky she was to have such a secret; her very own magic pony. She rubbed the sleep from her eyes and glanced at the clock on the shelf.

"Hello," said the pony amiably, not seeming to mind that he only just fitted the space between the bed and the wall.

"Ned," said Natty. "It's half-past two in the morning. Why aren't you asleep?"

"Now what sort of a greeting is that?" asked the pony. "Do you want me to go back in my picture?"

"No," said Natty, alarmed that he might. Ever since buying this most unusual pony poster from Cosby's Magic Emporium, Natty never quite knew when Ned would come alive. If the magic was happening now she didn't want to waste a moment of it. "It's only that it's the middle of the night. I've never been awake at half-past two in the morning before."

"That's the whole point," said Ned. "Everyone in the house is fast asleep, even that cat."

Ned meant Tabitha, Natty's tabby cat, who lay curled up on the duvet. This wasn't quite true, for Natty's wriggling had disturbed her and Tabitha had half an eye open. As for Ned, whether big or small, and he could be either, Tabitha had learnt to ignore him.

"It's the perfect time for jumping practice. So get up and get on."

During the day, when her curtains were drawn open, Natty often watched Penelope Potter jump her pony Pebbles over the blue barrels in the field on the other side of the lane. And now Ned was teaching her to do the same! What did it matter if it was the middle of the night? Natty scrambled from under the duvet, leaving Tabitha to curl into an undisturbed ball.

"I can't ride in pyjamas. I'd better get my jeans on."

"No need for that," said Ned. And of course there wasn't, for the moment Natty sat on Ned's back, the magic would change her pyjamas into riding clothes.

"Where shall we jump?" Natty asked, putting her bare toes into the waiting stirrup and springing on. The pony's reply was drowned in a rushing wind and Natty closed her eyes. When she opened them again, Ned was trotting across a field of brown tuffets which Natty recognized as her carpet. Ned's magic had shrunk them into the 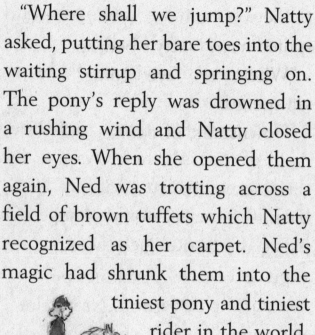 tiniest pony and tiniest rider in the world. He rounded the towering height of the door and cantered towards the top of the stairs, guided by the light that spilled from Natty's bedroom.

"Where are we going?" Natty whispered.

"Downstairs, of course," came the reply.

The drop from the landing on to the first stair was huge and the giant steps disappeared into a pit of black. Jumping practice was starting in earnest. Natty clung on, remembering she had gone downstairs like this once before. By the time they reached the hall Natty's eyes were staring pools, desperate to fathom out what lay ahead in the darkness. To her relief she hadn't fallen off. Just as well! Any loud noise would wake Mum, Dad and Jamie, and she certainly didn't want that.

"Get off now," said Ned. "And switch on the living-room light. We'll set up a jumping course in there."

"Oh, yes," said Natty. "I know the very place." She slid to the ground and let go of the reins. The wind spun her until she was her proper size and back in her pyjamas. She tiptoed forward, following the tiny Ned who cantered in front of her as if he were Esmerelda, Prince or

Percy, one of her three china horses come to life. She pushed open the living-room door and switched on the light. Fred the goldfish fluttered into action in his bowl on the shelf, surprised by the sudden brightness. Natty hurried to the table. It was laid ready for breakfast, just how Mum liked it.

"Ned, let's make a jumping course up here. There's loads of things that could be jumps."

"Show me." Natty held out her palms and lifted him.

Ned was soon trotting across the tablecloth, inspecting the breakfast crockery.

"Yes," he said. "The brown sauce bottle, the knives and forks and the salt and pepper pots. We can use all those."

"And the mugs," said Natty. "They can lie on their sides and be pretend barrels. Almost as good as the barrels Penelope Potter has for Pebbles to jump."

"They'll make a mighty jump, mind," said Ned, trotting round one. "The plates are no use. They need to be put to one side."

"My school bag's here," said Natty, grabbing it from beside a chair and delving in. "My pens and pencils can be poles."

She scattered three felt-tips and two striped pencils on the table and pulled out her scissors. "What can my scissors be? I know, they can be opened out and balanced on their handles. They're blunt as anything so no chance of getting cut – and brilliant as a cross-blade jump. And look, Mum's work-basket is loaded with cotton reels. They can be jump stands."

"Good thinking," said Ned. "As our small selves we'll practise indoors on the table, and as our large selves we'll ride out to Penelope Potter's field and jump Pebbles's barrels."

"In the dark?" exclaimed Natty, already balancing a knife and a fork across the salt and pepper pots.

"It's a full moon tonight," said Ned. "With luck we'll have plenty of light."

Natty darted to the window and pulled back the curtains, knowing Penelope would hate someone else jumping her blue barrels, even if it was in the dark. So she mustn't find out. Natty shielded her eyes and looked into the garden. Through a gap in the ballooning clouds, a round moon flooded silver light across the grass.

"If the clouds clear away it'll be perfect," Natty said, looking for stars. How exciting it would be to do night-time jumping out of doors. She returned to the table.

After the salt and pepper pot, knife and fork jump she opened the scissors and balanced them on their handles to make the cross-blade jump. The mugs were put on their sides and turned into barrels, and the cotton reels were stacked at three different heights. Two of the pens and one of the pencils became the poles, making the pen and pencil staircase.

Next she turned the sauce bottle on its side to make a wall. And finally, Natty discovered Mum's glasses in the work-basket, opened them out and made three jumps. The spectacles single, if jumped facing the lenses or the spectacles double if the arms were jumped. She bounced over them with her fingers – boing boing! Then she watched enchanted as Ned, mane flying, jumped the whole course.

It was a clear round and Natty hugged her hands to stop herself from clapping – a thing certain to wake the family and bring them downstairs to find out what was going on. Instead her delight was shown by a grin which grew wider as Ned trotted towards her. Leaning back on his haunches, he bowed politely.

"Now it's your turn, Natty. I'll come down to the floor, then you can mount. But we'll need some sort of road to ride up to get us back up here as our small selves."

"I know," said Natty. "If I pull Dad's chair close to the table we can use the rug."

She hurried to show Ned what she meant. After a bit of a struggle, she had the armchair in position with the rug draped over. One end hung from the chair back while Natty stretched the other end out over the seat and weighted it with the legs of the small table.

Now there was a long ramp from the floor to the top of the chair.

"Well done," said Ned, impressed. He jumped on to the rug and galloped all the way down to the floor without there being the slightest sag.

When his feet touched the carpet he was suddenly his big self, wearing saddle and bridle, and filling a large part of the room. Natty squeezed between Ned and the table and took hold of the reins. The moment she sprang into the saddle the mighty wind blew.

When it stopped she was dressed in her magic riding clothes and was dwarfed by giant furniture. Looking up, her breath was taken away by the vast armchair mountain.

Ned stepped on to the rug ramp cautiously, yet Natty's extra weight made no difference; the rug stayed taut and stretched. The pony trotted briskly all the way to the top and jumped on to the table.

Natty gasped at what she saw. As her big self she thought she had made the showjumps sensibly low; but now she was a tiny rider they looked huge. Most frightening of all were the giant mug barrels – imposingly round and solid and higher than Ned's shoulders.

"This is just the sort of practice course you need," said Ned. "Jump this lot and you'll soon be showing that Penelope Potter what's what."

"Yes," said Natty faintly. It seemed a flock of butterflies had been let loose in her tummy. Right now she didn't care if Penelope Potter could do showjumping better than she could. She wanted to go back to bed.

"Hold on tight," said Ned. Natty gulped, pulled nervously at the chin strap of her riding hat, then took a rein in each hand. Ned cantered towards the salt and pepper pot, knife and fork jump.

It was now or never, she could see that.

# Chapter 2

## Things That Go Bump in the Night

"Here we go," Ned said. At the last moment Natty grabbed a handful of mane. Ned soared into the air and, leaning into the angle of the jump, Natty went with him. Ned hit the tablecloth on the other side with a thump, and was cantering towards the open scissors cross-blade before Natty realized what was happening. The scissors were quickly behind them and Ned turned for the spectacles. It seemed strange cantering towards them, hardly possible that these glasses, so often perched on Mum's nose, were now as high as the stirrup irons.

"Don't worry about a thing," said Ned. "Just go with the jump." And he leapt. For a moment Natty caught a glimpse of Ned's legs reflected in the glass, then they were in the air and on the other side, cantering round to the sauce-bottle wall.

The sauce bottle seemed like nothing after the spectacles and even the pen and pencil staircase, which came next, was easy. Ned made a tight turn and suddenly the mug barrels lay ahead, by far the biggest jump. The pony gathered himself up, shortening his stride, and the barrels came closer. Natty concentrated hard and the moment Ned sprang she was ready. Ned cleared the barrels and so did she!

"Well done," he said. Natty was jubilant. It was a clear round.

"I didn't think I could do it but I did. Thank you, Ned." She leaned forward and gave the pony a hug.

"Now it's your turn to steer," said Ned. "You guide me to wherever you want to go."

"All right," said Natty, filled with a glorious sense of achievement. "We'll go round again."

So engrossed were they, that neither of them noticed the living-room door open just enough for a curious cat to pad silently in. Neither did they see Tabitha slip under the tablecloth to listen to the unusual thuds coming from above.

Although there was more to think about, Natty found steering fun, and with mounting excitement she turned Ned for the salt and pepper pot, knife and fork jump. They were quickly over it and cantering towards the scissors which they cleared easily, and the sauce-bottle wall, which caused no problems either.

After this, Natty changed the route and swung Ned round to jump the arms of the spectacles. Only when facing them did she realize this was going to be more tricky than she thought.

It was too late to stop. Ned jumped, hit the tablecloth and

jumped again. But it was too quick for Natty. By the second landing she had lost her balance. As Ned slowed to help her, the tablecloth suddenly shifted and an unexpected, furry giant landed in front of them.

"Stupid cat!" Ned shouted, swerving sharply. "Get off the table!"

Now nothing could stop Natty, and she and Ned parted company. In a split second Natty grew to her proper size and landed in the middle of the table. There was a terrible rattling of crockery and all the showjumps collapsed. Tabitha dived for the floor; Ned for the safety of the rug ramp. Unable to stop herself, Natty slid, pulling the tablecloth, breakfast things and showjumps off the table with her.

The crash and clatter was startling and landing with a surprised grunt amongst the debris, Natty sat stunned.

Then, from the corner of her eye, she saw the alarmed Fred swimming round and round in his bowl.

44

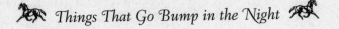 

"Sorry, Fred," she said. "No need to panic." Then she realized that after a crash like that there was every need to panic. She looked round quickly for Ned. Both he and Tabitha had disappeared. Just as well, she thought. Mindful that she had bare feet, she unwrapped herself from the tablecloth and hurriedly surveyed the damage.

It wasn't as bad as she expected. One plate in two halves, green felt-tip on the tablecloth, the handle of her own special mug snapped off. The rest a tangle that needed sorting. She started at once. With luck she could have the table set again before the mess was discovered. Working quickly, she started to pile up the plates and didn't see the tall, slow-moving figure creep in from the hall – with a big, black boot held up at the ready.

"Natty! What do you think you're doing?"

She nearly jumped out of her skin.

"Dad!" Behind Dad was Jamie, pale and wide-eyed, brandishing the magic wand from his conjuring set.

"You really frightened me!" she gasped.

"Us frighten *you*? What sort of a fright do you think you gave us? We thought you were a burglar. Your mother's under the duvet, all of a quiver," said Dad.

"No, I'm not," said Mum. "I just had to get my dressing-gown on." Even Mum was clasping a wooden coat-hanger to her chest. "I couldn't meet a burglar in my nightie."

"Oh." said Natty.

"Yes," said Jamie. "We were going to tie you up and hand you over to the police."

"Humph!" said Dad, dropping the boot in the hall. "That won't be necessary now we know it was you."

"I'm sorry to wake you," said Natty. "I had a bit of an accident with the tablecloth. Well, it was Tabitha. She got on the table and, well, her claws pulled it and, well, everything came off." It was the best truth she could manage and Natty hoped that it would do.

"But what were you doing down

here at this time of night?" Dad asked. "It's gone three o'clock. You should be fast asleep." Natty held up her broken mug with one hand and crossed her fingers behind her back with the other.

"I came to fetch a mug of water and now I've broken it. Sorry."

Fortunately Tabitha chose this moment to come out from behind the sofa and brush herself around Natty's legs.

"Honestly, that cat's more trouble than she's worth," said Mum. "Come on, we can leave the mess until morning. Back to bed everyone."

But Natty realized she couldn't leave everything until the morning. There were pens and pencils, cotton reels and scissors muddled in with the crockery. She needed to tidy them away to avoid anyone asking more awkward questions.

"Leave everything." Mum was firm. "Find a mug with a handle and fill it. Then it's straight up to bed."

Dad shook his head. "Accidents will happen, I suppose," he said.

"Excitement over, Jamie. Back to bed now. It's a school day tomorrow."

When Natty came from the kitchen carrying her water, she looked quickly round for Ned. He was nowhere to be seen, thank goodness, although she longed to know where he'd got to. Mum's hand on her shoulder steered her from the living room.

"Can we leave the door open for Tabitha?" Natty asked.

"I suppose so," said Mum, switching off the light. "Now upstairs at once. In future remember to take up water with you when you go to bed. We don't want a repeat performance of tonight, thank you very much."

Natty plodded up the stairs with her mug clasped in both hands. She stopped at the top.

"If I was a burglar would you have bashed me with the coat-hanger?"

With twinkling eyes, Mum waved it.

"If you'd been stealing my favourite flower vase – yes! Now hurry back to bed."

Natty turned into her bedroom and checked to see if Ned was back in his poster. He wasn't. She put the mug beside her clock, flopped on to the duvet with a sigh, and switched off the light. It's lucky Mum and Dad don't seem cross so far, she thought. But the kind of accident they *think* I've had is one thing.

Showjumping on the table is quite another. If they find *that* out, then they'll be cross. She covered her knees with the duvet.

When everyone had gone back to sleep she would find Ned and sort the showjumps from the rest of the crockery on the floor.

# Chapter 3
## The Moon Shines Bright

It was difficult trying to stay awake. Natty propped herself against the wall but soon her head nodded forward. When her chin knocked her chest she opened her eyes and shook herself, but the effect didn't last long. Her eyelids drooped and down went her chin again. This time she didn't wake.

It was Tabitha landing on the duvet, purring loudly and brushing her body against Natty's sagging knees that finally roused her.

"Mmm, mmm, what?" Slowly she awoke. "Tabby?" she said, and wrapped her arms around the warm furry bundle. The purring grew even louder. Natty would have dropped off again if Tabitha hadn't licked the back of her hand. The rasping sound and prickly sensation woke her properly, and remembering what she had to do she felt along the shelf for her pocket torch.

"This time, Tabby, you stay here," whispered Natty. She shone the torch at the clock. A quarter to four! Then on to Ned's poster. Empty. She listened hard and, although Tabitha was still purring, the rest of the house seemed quiet and still. She climbed cautiously out of bed, tiptoed to the window and lifted back the curtain.

The sky was full of stars and the field on the other side of the lane was flooded with moonlight.

Esmerelda, Prince and Percy stood in a line on the window-sill. They seemed to stare at the spot where Penelope Potter's pony Pebbles stood, head up, ears pricked, a shining silver statue in the middle of a silver lake. Natty craned her neck to see what he was looking at. Whatever it was was way out of view and she didn't dare open the window in case it made a noise.

She let the curtain fall; she had important things to see to. She squeezed round her bedroom door, and turning the handle bit by bit closed it without a sound, leaving Tabitha shut in. The torch lit her way along the landing and down the stairs.

Natty paused at the bottom and listened. Silence! More confident, she tiptoed into the living room. She pushed the door to and put on the light to see the tiny Ned canter across the carpet towards her.

"Are you ready to jump in Pebbles's field?" he asked. "The moon shines bright."

Natty longed to say yes, longed to ride out into the shimmering world of Pebbles's field, but first things had to come first.

"I can't," she said. "Not until I've tidied up the jumping things."

She put her torch in her pyjama bottoms pocket and started her search amongst the wreckage. She closed the scissors, grateful that she hadn't sat on them, and found the spectacles in one piece, which was a relief. She picked out the cotton reels and tidied them back into

Mum's work-basket, and the pens and pencils she shoved in her school bag. There was nothing she could do about the green blob of felt-tip on the tablecloth but it wasn't a very big blob, so with luck no one would notice it.

"There," said Natty. "All done. I'll have to leave the cutlery and other stuff on the floor otherwise it'll be obvious I got up again. Lucky no one noticed the rug over the chair. I could never have explained that." She laid it out carefully on the floor and pulled Dad's armchair back into place.

"It was unfortunate about that cat," said Ned. "The jumping was going well until she arrived."

"Never mind," said Natty. "She can't follow us this time. I've shut her in my bedroom."

"Good," said Ned. "You'd better put something on your feet."

"My wellies! They're by the back door. Let's go out that way and round by the side gate."

Natty switched out the light and with the torch, shone the way to the kitchen. Here she pulled on her wellington boots and unlocked the back door.

The tiny pony jumped from the step and Natty followed him out into the night.

Nothing stirred. A barn owl hooted in Winchway Wood and above them twinkled a million distant stars. But most enchanting of all, Natty thought, was to see Ned, standing before her on the grass, a proper pony size, tacked up and ready for her to mount.

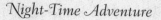 

Showjumping by moonlight! What could be more thrilling?

"Penelope Potter'd be furious if she found out I'd used her jumps without asking," whispered Natty, as with shining eyes she took hold

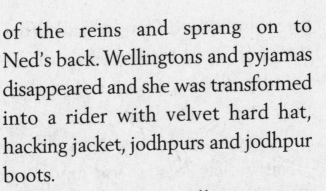

of the reins and sprang on to Ned's back. Wellingtons and pyjamas disappeared and she was transformed into a rider with velvet hard hat, hacking jacket, jodhpurs and jodhpur boots.

"Penelope Potter will never ever find out," whispered back Ned.

How silly to think that in such wonderful clothes and riding such a handsome chestnut pony that Penelope Potter had a chance of recognizing her. Of course she didn't.

Natty chuckled with excitement as Ned walked across the grass and round the side of the house to the gate. She leaned forward and lifted the latch. Ned backed away so she could pull the gate open and then they were in the lane.

"Ready to go?" asked Ned.

Natty was ready for anything, which was just as well. For instead of letting Natty open the field gate, Ned trotted a little way down the lane, turned and cantered straight for it. He put in a huge leap and they were in the field before the gasp of surprise had left Natty's lips.

"Well sat," said Ned. "In spite of that unfortunate tumble earlier I can see that you haven't lost your nerve."

"You didn't give me a chance to think about it," said Natty.

"After the gate, jumping Pebbles's barrels will be nothing." And her eyes searched the field for the dappled grey pony. "That's funny. Where is Pebbles? He was here a little while ago. I saw him from my window."

"Well, he's not here now," said Ned.
With a jolt Natty remembered
Pebbles's fixed look in the
direction of Penelope's stable yard,
and felt a sudden stab of anxiety.

Across the still night air and from
the direction of the yard came the
long, lonely whinny of a confused
and worried pony. It was answered
by a voice Natty had never heard
before. Its low, cross tones struck a
chill in her heart. She could just
make out the words.

"Get on in horse, else you'll
regret it."

# Chapter 4
## Thieves in the Night

Above the stable roof, the moonlight lit up the flat top of a lorry. Natty froze with fear, but Ned hurried into action and she clung on.

"Don't say a word," he whispered, and keeping in the shadow of the hedge, they trotted towards

Penelope's stable yard, Ned's unshod feet swishing through the grass, beating out a soft rhythm. From the yard came the hollow clatter of pony feet climbing up a horsebox ramp.

Natty knew the sound from when Penelope loaded Pebbles into his pony trailer, only this time it wasn't Penelope. Penelope was tucked up fast asleep in bed. Someone else was loading Pebbles; someone up to no good.

"We've got to stop them," she whispered in Ned's ear. "They're stealing Pebbles!"

"Don't worry," Ned whispered back. "We will." And he broke into a steady canter, charging through the open gate into the stable yard where he galloped towards the lorry and straight into a rushing wind. Ned and Natty went from big to small in a moment and disappeared between the front wheels of the lorry just as a pair of trousered legs ran alongside it.

"What was that?" The cross voice again. "I swear there was only one pony in the field. Was that another?"

Now a younger voice.

"No boss, I didn't see anything."

"Close up the ramp and get in the cab. We got to clear out of here. That grey animal's made noise enough to wake the dead."

One pair of legs disappeared towards the front of the lorry, the other pair ran for the back. Ned galloped from between the rear wheels, swung round and jumped on to the ramp. Up he galloped, leaping each anti-slip bar like a racehorse, his rider bent double like a jockey. Natty glanced over her shoulder in time to see the accomplice thief start lifting.

The ramp straightened under them and Ned half-jumped, half-fell into the lorry. It banged closed behind them and they were left in pitch black. Pebbles, upset by the rough treatment he had received, cried out with an ear-splitting whinny that only faded when the engine broke into a roar. The lorry swung out of the yard and drove off, nearly knocking Ned from his feet.

"Natty, are you all right?" Ned asked, his sides heaving as he regained his breath.

"Yes, but I can't see a thing." Wondering if her torch would have transferred itself from her pyjamas to her jodhpurs, she fumbled in the little pocket near the waistband. What a relief to find it was there!

"Shine it ahead," said Ned. "I need to see where Pebbles's feet are."

The wobbly pinprick of light picked out Pebbles's four great hooves, one after the other, enabling Ned to make his way shakily across the juddering rubber matting.

"Got my bearings now," said Ned. "Hold tight and crouch right down."

A whirl of wind spun them and in a moment Ned was as big as Pebbles and Natty found herself ducking down just below the lorry's roof. Pebbles peered into the torchlight with a look of surprise.

"It's all right, Pebbles. It's only us," said Natty. "I'm going to get off Ned and untie you." Pebbles whickered with relief; friends had arrived.

"Easy does it, Natty," said Ned.

"And keep hold of my reins." Natty slid to the ground between the two ponies, who now stood side by side. She looped Ned's reins over her arm and edged towards Pebbles's head. Ned rested his muzzle in a comforting way on the grey pony's neck while Natty untied the halter rope. As soon as he could, Pebbles nuzzled Natty's arm before turning to Ned. The two ponies blew a nose-to-nose greeting in the way that horses do.

"Now what?" asked Natty, grabbing a handful of Ned's mane as the lorry lurched round a bend.

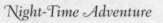

"We get the thieves to stop," said
Ned. "And we do it like this."

To Natty's surprise Ned's back

end lifted into the air and both hind legs kicked hard against the side of the lorry. Everything swayed.

As if this was his cue, Pebbles did the same and to greater effect because he wore metal shoes. The lorry jerked and swayed and Natty held fast to the tying-up ring. Bang and bang and bang went four pony feet. The metal kicking-plate buckled and above it the wood splintered. There were angry shouts from the driver's cab. The ponies renewed their efforts. Gasping and puffing they put all their energy into knocking a big hole.

The lorry came to a spluttering, lurching stop and the floor ended up angled to one side.

"Looks like we've ended up in a ditch," said Ned cheerily, as if he couldn't have wished for anything better. "Get on, Natty, and get ready to lead Pebbles down the ramp."

Pebbles, meanwhile, kept up the kicking with one leg, needing his other three to balance. Natty had just enough space. It was the first time she had mounted from this side, and using her right foot was awkward until she found herself pushed from underneath by Ned's nose.

Once in the saddle she crouched low to avoid hitting her head on the roof. She had a firm hold of Pebbles's lead rope with one hand; the other held tight to Ned's mane. This was the most scary thing she had ever done and she took a deep breath to quieten her pounding heart.

Bang and bang and bang, went Pebbles. Chunks of wood flew and there were angry shouts at the back of the lorry.

"Get ready," said Ned, turning to face the ramp. "As soon as this thing goes down we leave."

The lock unclicked. Bang, bang went Pebbles for good measure. A slit of moonlight appeared and the ramp started to go down. Pebbles got in two more kicks and Ned coiled under Natty like a spring.

"All right, you stupid horse," said a brawny figure, springing towards them. "You've asked for it."

"Charge!" yelled Natty at the top of her voice and Ned leapt forwards. The astonished horse thief tumbled backwards.

Natty had the satisfaction of seeing him splash into the ditch as Ned clattered down the chaotically bouncing ramp, followed by an eager Pebbles. Then with a sound like gunfire, a hinge snapped. The terrified accomplice dived for the safety of the hedge as not one pony but two jumped to safety and cantered off down the moonlit road.

"That's given them something to think about," said Ned. "Stuck in a ditch with the ramp hanging half off. The lorry won't be going anywhere like that. It's well and truly stranded."

"Good," grinned the triumphant Natty, holding tight to Pebbles's lead rope. "They won't be stealing any more ponies tonight, that's for sure."

Behind them furious shouts faded into the distance.

# Chapter 5

## *Mystery Rider*

Pebbles's hooves hammered the road's hard surface and mingled with the duller beat of Ned's unshod feet. The further they raced, the more Natty was sure a beat was missing. But there was nothing wrong with Pebbles – he cantered easily beside her – and

Ned was fine too. In the end Natty forgot to listen as she tried to work out where they were.

The ponies put in a good distance between themselves and the stranded thieves before slowing. Hot and blowing, they stopped for a rest. The moon seemed to shed less light and the sky was paler. Natty wondered how long they had been travelling and how far they had come.

"Well," said Ned. "Where do we go from here?"

"I'm not sure!" Natty tried desperately to find a recognizable landmark. But the moonlit countryside looked so different from how she usually saw it. "We haven't gone by any turnings so we must have come along this road in the lorry. Best to carry on until I work it out."

The ponies started walking and the uneven sound from Pebbles's feet – three clops and a pat – became obvious. Natty finally understood the problem.

"Pebbles has lost a shoe!"

"Wrenched off with all that kicking, no doubt," said Ned. "It's lucky he's not gone lame." But there was no sign of Pebbles limping. On the contrary, he pulled to go forward. Ahead, the moon hung above a line of dark trees, and behind them was a spire.

"I know where we are!" cried Natty, and she realized Pebbles did too. "Not far from home. This is our village. That's the church."

They set off at a trot, coming into Main Street, clattering past the shop, the petrol station and the bus-stop. All familiar signs of home.

"Here's our lane," said Natty. "That's the front entrance to Penelope's house." She pointed to a smart white gate facing on to the main road. "But mostly the Potters use the other entrance. The back drive that comes out opposite the stable yard. The once-upon-a-time stables behind the house are garages now. That's why Pebbles has a new stable in his field."

They swung into the lane and Natty had high hopes of being able to turn Pebbles out without anyone seeing them. But torchlight suddenly lit up the lane and two figures emerged from the Potters' back drive.

"Now what are we going to do?" she whispered. "It's Mr Potter and Penelope. They've heard us coming."

"Talk your way out of it. You can do it," whispered back Ned.

"What happens if they recognize me?"

"They won't," Ned assured her.

"Excuse me, that's my pony you've got there!" said Penelope, arms outstretched to stop them passing. "Hand him over."

"That's enough, Penelope. Just leave this to me," said Mr Potter.

"Now, young lady. What are you doing with my daughter's pony, and what for that matter are you doing out at this time of night?"

Natty leaned down and dropped Pebbles's halter rope into Penelope's waiting hand. "I was bringing him back. He's been stolen."

"We know that," said Penelope. "I heard him whinnying. I saw the thieves' lorry drive off up the lane."

Mr Potter looked puzzled.

"How did you find him?" he asked. "The police are out searching right now."

Terrified they'd recognize her voice, the words tumbled out in a rush.

"He escaped from the horsebox. It's stuck in a ditch with a broken ramp. Turn left at the top of the lane and keep on till you find it. Tell the police that. Oh, and he's lost a back shoe." Her legs gave Ned a squeeze. "Goodbye." Ned sprang forwards.

"Now just a minute, young lady," cried Mr Potter, but he was distracted by Pebbles trying to go with them. Mr Potter had to help Penelope hang on tight and in doing so neither of them saw Ned turn at

Natty's house and jump the side gate. The girl rider and the pony had vanished by the time Pebbles was calm again.

Quickly, Ned reached the back garden and Natty slid from his back.

"Thank you, Ned, for saving Pebbles and for the wonderful indoor showjumping." She gave him a quick hug and let go of the reins. At once she was back in her pyjamas and wellies.

She pushed the back door open. Ned tossed his mane and in a moment was his tiny self, leaping up the doorstep into the house. Natty hurried after him, locking the door and kicking off her boots as she went. She caught Ned up on the landing, highlighting him in her torch beam as he pranced, waiting for her.

"Goodbye, Natty, until next time." The tiny pony voice was a drift of tinkling bells.

"Goodbye, Ned. It's been the most exciting night of my life!" came her whispered reply. She pushed open her bedroom door and the miniature pony galloped ahead.

By the time Natty had crept inside, Ned was safely back in his poster. She switched off her torch. Daylight was creeping between her curtains; it was nearly morning. She wriggled her feet under the sleeping Tabitha and looked up at Ned's picture.

"Night night, Magic Pony," she sighed.

"I hope next time will be soon." And she lay down. She sat up again almost at once. "How typical! Penelope didn't even say thank you."

Then, with a sigh of exhaustion, she flopped down again. The next thing she knew she was being shaken awake by Jamie.

"Mum says you've got to get up now," he said. "What's the matter with you? Why didn't you wake up? She's called and called. Now you've missed breakfast."

"Why? What time is it?"

"Quarter to eight!" said Jamie and left her groaning. Natty thought she must be the weariest person in the world. She looked up at Ned in his poster, and slowly the details of last night's adventure came back: showjumping on the table, the shambles on the living-room floor, and saving Pebbles. Tabitha slid off the bed, stretched and trotted off to find her breakfast.

Natty staggered out of bed and, after flinging on her school clothes, arrived in the kitchen with enough time to grab her lunch-box.

"About time too, Natty," said Mum, handing it over. "I've put an extra sandwich in for you to eat on the bus. Now hurry."

"Thanks, Mum." Natty grabbed her school bag from the living room and ran.

She turned the corner at the end of the lane, and saw Penelope talking excitedly to Jamie by the school bus-stop and, for once, he appeared to be listening.

"Amazing," she heard him say as she drew close. "Hey, Natty, guess what happened to Pebbles?"

"I'll tell if you don't mind, Jamie," said Penelope. "He is my pony."

"What?" asked Natty, pretending not to know.

"In the middle of the night he got stolen!" Before Natty could think how to react Penelope went on. "It was weird. We got him back again. But not from the police. From this mystery rider. We heard ponies coming down the lane and there was this girl, terribly smart, on a super chestnut, leading Pebbles.

She told us where the thieves' lorry was, handed Pebbles over and vanished! And she was right. The police caught the thieves trying to pull their lorry out of a ditch with a stolen tractor. Only nobody seems to know who she was. Don't you think that's extraordinary?"

Natty blinked and nodded.

"Yes, and another amazing thing. The thieves tried to say they hadn't stolen Pebbles. But the police found his lost shoe in their lorry and then they got terribly confused about whether they'd stolen one pony or two. All rather peculiar, don't you think?"

Natty opened her mouth to reply, but was saved from having to by the arrival of the school bus. The three of them climbed aboard and Natty sank thankfully into a seat, grateful her secret was safe and delighted the thieves had been caught. Now Penelope had a new audience for her story and told it all over again to anyone on the bus who would listen. At the next stop, Penelope's special friend Trudi got on, so she had to be told too. Left alone, Natty smiled quietly to herself, ate her sandwich and made up an exciting pretend to keep herself awake.

In it she and Ned soared over Pebbles's blue barrels at last.

## The End

# Magic Pony

Natty's and Ned's adventures do
not stop here! Read the other
books in the series, and make sure
you don't miss the next time Ned
jumps out of his magic poster. . .

# Magic Pony

### The
### Champion Jumper
Elizabeth Lindsay

# Magic Pony

Summer Special

*Seaside*
*Detectives*
Elizabeth Lindsay

SCHOLASTIC